Willy's Silly Grandma

story by
CYNTHIA DeFELICE
pictures by
SHELLEY JACKSON

ORCHARD BOOKS
NEW YORK

Orchard Books, 95 Madison Avenue, New York, NY 10016

Manufactured in the United States of America

Printed by Barton Press, Inc.

Bound by Horowitz/Rae

10   9   8   7   6   5   4   3   2   1

The text of this book is set in 16 point Galliard.

The illustrations are ink and crayon reproduced in full color.

Library of Congress Cataloging-in-Publication Data

DeFelice, Cynthia C.

Willy's silly grandma / story by Cynthia DeFelice ;

pictures by Shelley Jackson.

p.   cm.

"A Richard Jackson book"—Half t.p.

Summary: Willy doesn't believe in any of his grandmother's superstitions, until he ventures down by the Big Swamp one dark night and comes to realize how smart Grandma is.

ISBN 0-531-30012-9. — ISBN 0-531-33012-5 (lib. bdg.)

[1. Grandmothers—Fiction.   2. Superstition—Fiction.]

I. Jackson, Shelley, ill.   II. Title.

PZ7.D3597Wi   1997   [E]—dc20   96-42287

For Frances Temple,
who knew what she knew
~ C.DeF.

There once was a little boy named Willy who lived with his lovin' daddy and his lovin' grandma.

Now, Willy's grandma believed in magic and she knew how it worked. Said her mama had told her, and her mama's mama had told her, so she knew what she knew. But when she told Willy about magic, he just laughed.

"Silly Grandma!" he said. "There's no such thing."

Willy's grandma believed in lucky charms. She kept a rabbit's foot in her pocket, a horseshoe nailed over the door, and a four-leaf clover pressed between the pages of a book, all to bring good luck.

"Good luck, my foot!" said Willy.

Willy's grandma could tell you what kind of winter was coming, how to make your sweetheart love you back, and how to cure all manner of aches and pains and ailments, even warts.

"Why's Grandma so silly?" Willy asked his daddy. "She told me, if I want my cold to go away, I'd better kiss a mule!"

"Now, Willy," said his daddy, "don't you go calling your grandma silly. She's my mama, and she raised me up, and I can tell you this for true: your grandma's not silly. She's a little superstitious, but when it comes to the things that matter, your grandma's brighter than a star and sharper than a porcupine quill. Your grandma knows what she knows."

But Willy still thought Grandma was silly.

Well, one Sunday afternoon Willy's lovin' grandma said, "Willy, did I ever tell you it's awful bad luck to cut your toenails on a Sunday?"

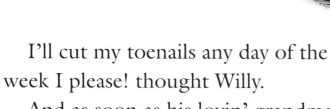

I'll cut my toenails any day of the week I please! thought Willy.

And as soon as his lovin' grandma wasn't looking, Willy got out the big old kitchen scissors and cut his toenails—*snip, snap, clip!*

He waited, but nothing bad happened.

Clip, snip, snap! He cut some more.

But nothing bad happened, nothing at all.

"Silly Grandma,"
he said.

On Monday morning his lovin' grandma told him, "Willy, don't you go singing a song, now, until *after* you've had your breakfast. You know what they say: sing before breakfast and you'll cry before supper."

Singing before breakfast ain't nothing! thought Willy.

And as soon as his lovin' grandma stepped outside, Willy sang a song about Froggy going courting, every single verse.

He sang the whole song over again, and another song, too. But supper came and supper went and nothing bad happened, nothing at all.

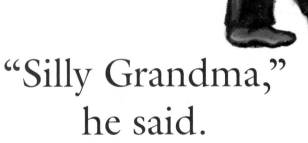

"Silly Grandma," he said.

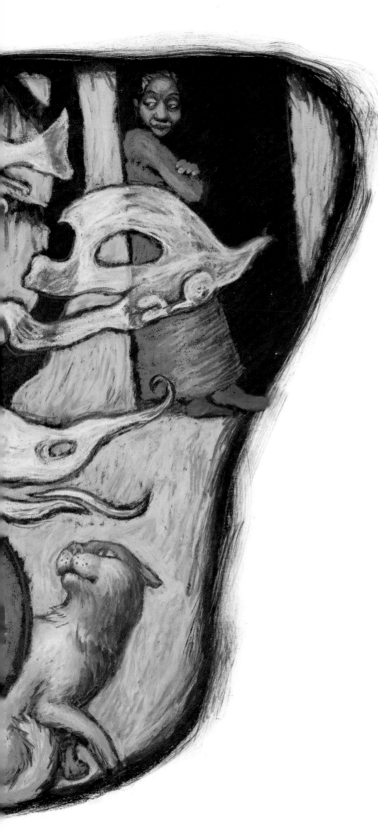

On Tuesday his lovin' grandma said, "Willy, don't ever put your hat down on the bed, no sir. A hat on the bed is the worst kind of bad luck."

Hat on the bed, hat on your head, it makes no nevermind, thought Willy.

And when his grandma turned around, Willy put his summer straw hat *and* his winter wool cap right down in the center of his bed.

He watched and he waited and he sat and he stared . . . but nothing bad happened, nothing at all.

"Silly Grandma," he said.

On Wednesday his lovin' grandma told him, "Don't ever go
walking around with one shoe on and one shoe off, Willy.
Why, if you do that, you'll have you some wearisome worries."

One shoe, two shoes, barefoot—makes no difference nohow! thought Willy.

And the very instant his grandma went inside the house, Willy took his left shoe off, kept his right shoe on, and walked around just everywhere he pleased.

He walked all the way down the road and back . . . but nothing bad happened, nothing at all.

"Silly Grandma," he said.

On Thursday his lovin' grandma said, "Willy, don't you ever try to count the stars, you hear? 'Cause it surely does bring bad luck if you do."

Who wants to count stars anyhow? thought Willy.

But that very night, as soon as it got dark, where was Willy? Lying on the front porch, counting the stars.

"Five hundred six, five hundred seven, five hundred eight . . ."

He counted all the way to one thousand and one . . . and nothing bad happened, nothing at all.

"Silly Grandma," he said.

On Friday his lovin' grandma told him, "Don't ever bring the ax or the hoe into the house, Willy, unless you're looking for some real bad luck."

I'll bring the ax *and* the hoe inside if I've a mind to! thought Willy.

And as soon as his lovin' grandma went to town, Willy went out to the barn, got the ax, got the hoe, and brought them both inside the house.

But nothing bad happened, nothing at all.

He asked his daddy again, "Why's Grandma so silly? She told me if my stomach hurts I should lie down with a penny in my belly button! She said to put a knife under the bed to cut the pain in two!"

"I've told you and told you not to call your grandma silly," said his daddy. "When it comes to the things that matter, Willy, I'll tell you for true: your grandma knows what she knows."

"Hmmmph," said Willy. "In a pig's eye!"

On Saturday his lovin' grandma said, "Willy, don't you go walking by the Big Swamp at night. Something could give you a fearsome fright."

I ain't afraid to go walking by the swamp, day or night or in between! thought Willy.

And, that very night, where was little Willy? All by himself, walking through the marsh mud down by the Big Swamp, in the dark.

He wasn't scared, not Willy.

"Silly Grandma," he said, right out loud.

Mist rose from the still, black water and touched the back of Willy's neck like a chilly finger. But he wasn't scared, not Willy.

Something he couldn't see flew right past his face. "It's only a bat," whispered Willy. "I think. . . ."

An owl hooted, sad and mournful as could be. "But I'm n-not sc-cared," said Willy.

Dry leaves skittered past Willy's feet, making sounds like footsteps.

Or—were there footsteps?
    There—behind him?
        Willy didn't want to look.
            He was sure there were footsteps.

                Coming closer.
Then,
        he heard a M O A N ,
            and a G R O A N ,
                then a W A I L
                    (Willy grew pale).
        Something S C R E E C H E D ,
            fingers R E A C H E D ,
                lights F L I C K E R E D . . .
                    S O M E T H I N G   S N I C K E R E D . . . .

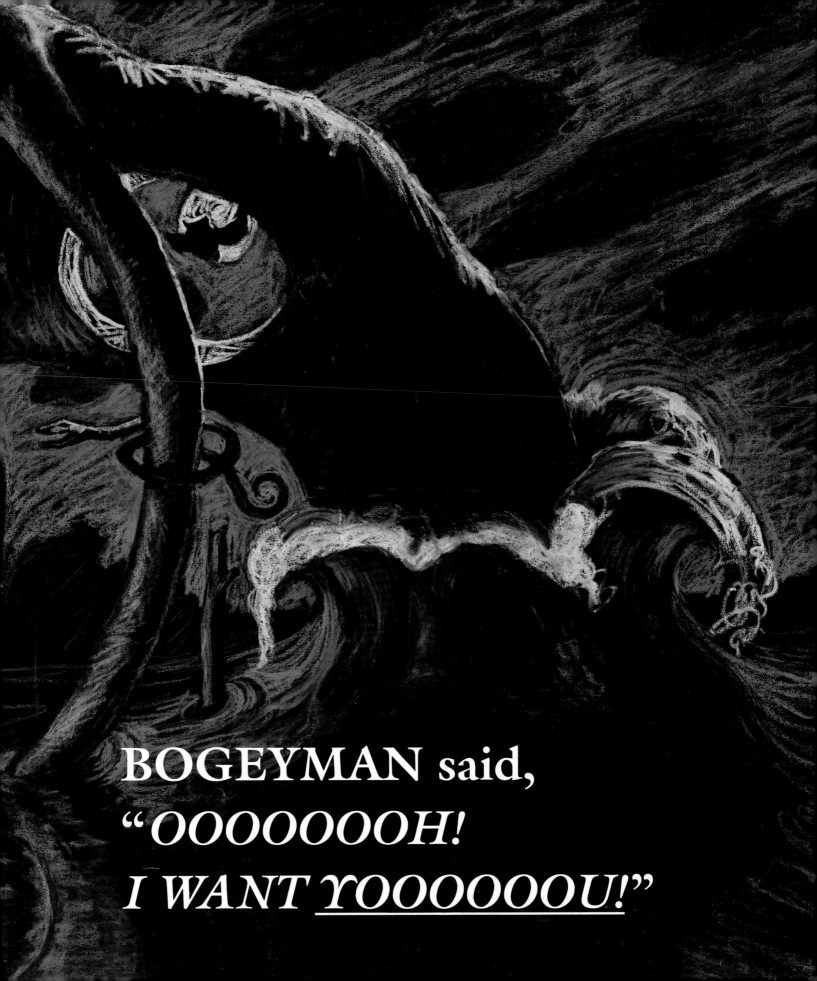

BOGEYMAN said,
"OOOOOOOH!
I WANT YOOOOOOU!"

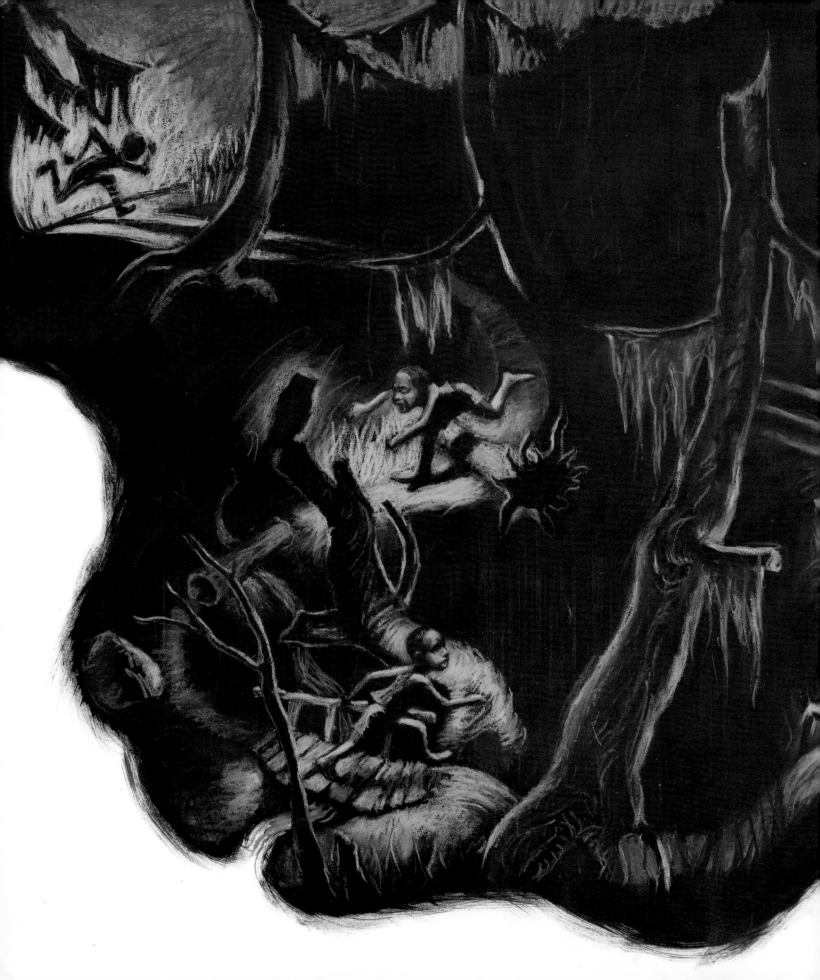

Little Willy began to run.

He ran   "GRANDMA!"
    and he ran   "GRANDMA!"
        and he ran   "GRANDMA!"
            and he ran   "GRANDMA!"
                and he ran   "GRANDMA!"

until he was safe at home in his lovin' grandma's arms.

"Willy, my Willy, what's wrong?" she asked. "You're all a-quiver and a-tremble."

"Grandma, I was walking by the Big Swamp and there were *moans* and *groans* and *wails*!"

Grandma rocked Willy and held him tight. "That was just the wind whistling a song for my Willy," she said.

"There were fingers reaching for me, Grandma!" cried little Willy.

"It was only the willow branches trying to tickle my Willy," said Grandma.

"There were lights that flickered, Grandma!"

"Those were the stars winking at my Willy," said Grandma.

"There was a *bogeyman*, Grandma! He wanted to *get* me!"

"Oh, it surely does seem that way, doesn't it, when you're walking down by the Big Swamp at night," said Grandma. "I know—I've been there myself. But there's no bogeyman, little Willy, I can tell you that for true."

"For true, Grandma?"

"For true, Willy."

Grandma held Willy and rocked him in her lovin' arms and sang him the songs she used to sing to Willy's daddy way back when. And soon little Willy was sound asleep.

'Cause, after all, when it came to the bogeyman,
Willy's grandma knew what she knew.